THE NINCOMPOOP WHO SPILLED HER SOUP!

STORY: RICH DRAKE
ART: CATHY CHRISTY O'CONNOR
ART DIRECTION: BERNARD O'CONNOR

2.

t all started with a...

giggle!

It's about five years ago now that I flew over to England to spend some much-needed vacation time with my two sons, my daughter-in-law and my little granddaughter.

A few days into my visit, still recovering from jet lag, I found myself stretched out on my son's living room couch snoring away, when I heard someone fiddling with the front door lock. With my heart racing, I sat bolt upright just as my granddaughter and daughter-in-law entered the room.

"Go ahead, tell PopPop what happened at school today." My granddaughter stepped forward and said: "My teacher said that our class was acting like little Nincompoops".

And then came the giggles and then more giggles; they just wouldn't stop. Over the course of the next week, when there was a break in any conversation, I would work in the word Nincompoop somehow for the benefit of my granddaughter, and the result was always the same: more giggling.

The evening before my departure, I headed up the stairs to read my granddaughter one last bedtime story. And so I did just that. But when I leaned over to give her a big hug and a kiss, I could see that she just wasn't her usual happy self. "Do you really have to leave tomorrow, PopPop? Yes, I have to leave. But that doesn't mean I want to leave." Realizing that this had gone over her head, I reached over and took the book from her bed that I had just read to her.

See this book. Well, PopPop is going to write a special book just for you. And do you know what it's going to be called?" "What, PopPop"?

"The Little Nincompoop" "How's that sound"? She wasn't giggling. But at least she was smiling. And then something magical happened. I said:

"There was a little Nincompoop, who used a fork to eat her soup, it seemed the more soup that she ate, the more soup landed on her plate."

Where those words came from, I have no idea, even to this day. But I do know this: they became the first four lines of the book that you now hold in your hands. The rest of the words were written on my flight back home to New York the following day.

But as for the beautiful illustrations, they were provided nearly five years later (and it was well worth the wait) by two extraordinarily talented artists that I'm also happy to call my friends: Bernie and Cathy O'Connor. Thank you.

I would also like to thank my three children: Dave, Devon and Ian for all their support and suggestions along the way. But mostly, I want to thank my three grandchildren (those lovable Nincompoops): Ellana, Cullen and Isla, whose wide-eyed sense of wonder, achingly beautiful innocence and infectious laughter inspire me each-and-every day of my life.

Rich Drake

There was a silly Nincompoop
Who used a fork to eat her soup
It seems the more soup that she ate
The more soup landed on her plate

5

She took the straw out of her cup
She sipped her soup and sucked it up

Then after one last sloppy slurp
The Nincompoop began to burp

Her father said: "That's not polite!
You're acting very rude tonight."

The Nincompoop said: "Sorry, dad;
I didn't mean to make you mad

But daddy, you were also rude
You talked to me while chewing food

And you spit gravy on my shirt
Now just for that there's...

Her mother looked at her and smiled
Then said: "You are a clever child

But you should learn to hold your tongue
You're very fresh for one so young"

"Hold my tongue? Don't make me giggle
It's slippery and it likes to wiggle

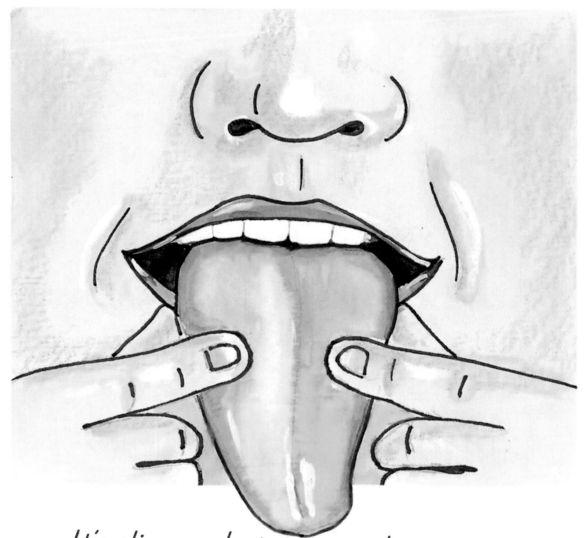

It's slimy and it's squirmy too
To hold my tongue's too hard to do"

Her father said: "Now that's enough
I've had it with this silly stuff

And all your giggly gobbledygook
Stop acting like a Nincompoop!

Now eat your veggies and your meat
There's plenty there for you to eat
And no more talking, sit up straight
I want to see you clean your plate"

"I'll clean my plate, dad, if you wish
But all my food's still on my dish
To clean my plate would be a waste

Before I even had one taste"
Her father said: "I've heard it all
You're going to drive me up a wall"

The Nincompoop said: "If you'd like
I'll go outside and get my bike
And then I'll drive you up the wall
But hold on tight or you might fall"

Her father got up from his chair
And started pulling out his hair
He took a deep breath, then he said:
"I think it's time you went to bed

20

Now go upstairs and go to sleep
And I don't want to hear a peep"

The Nincompoop began to laugh
"Sometimes I might peep in my bath
But I don't peep in bed no more
I haven't done that since I'm four"

Her mother said: "Go to your room
Your dad and I will be there soon
And pick your toys up off the floor
That's what you have a toy box for"

AND NO MORE
GIBBERISH
from you
So get a move on
Scoot! Skidoo!

24

But when her parents came upstairs
Her blocks and dolls were piled on chairs
The Nincompoop was in her bed
But she was standing on her head

"Hey mom! Hey dad! You're upside down"
Her father said: "Don't be a clown!
It's time for sleep and not for play
Tomorrow is another day"

The Nincompoop sat up in bed
She raised her eyebrows as she said:
"Oh that's a silly thing to say
Tomorrow's more than just a day

There's also tomorrow night
Now am I wrong or am I right?"
But soon her eyes began to droop
She was one tired Nincompoop

Her parents tiptoed out the door
Was she asleep? They weren't sure
But when they saw the bouncing ball
They heard their little daughter call

"Tomorrow morning, see you then
We'll get to do this all again!"

Nighty - night!

DID YOU FIND ALL THESE HIDDEN WORDS?

FORK	MISCHIEF
SOUP	BIRD
STRAW	BALL
DAD	BEAR
SPILL	WOW
PEAS	MOM

Before you peek at the answers below, why not look through the book again to see if you can find them all.

ANSWERS:

(FORK - PG. 5) (SOUP & STRAW - PG. 6) (DAD - PG. 10) (SPILL - PG. 13) (PEAS - PG. 16) (MISCHIEF - PG.18) (BIRD - PG.19) (BALL - PG. 23) (BEAR - PG.25) (WOW is easy, PG. 26, but you have to turn the book upside down to find MOM)

Made in United States
North Haven, CT
20 November 2021

11293174R00020